THE ROCK PEOPLE

We have heartfelt gratitude for our family and friends who encouraged and supported us to bring the Rock People to life on these pages. We'd also like to thank: Andy Azula for providing a vision for the Rock People; Emma Walton Hamilton and Mary-Catherine Harrison for their astute story-telling editing; Don Werthmann and Michael Bostic for their creative critiques and editing; Kristine Willimann for book layout; Luke Bostic for photographic contribution; Chris Murdoch, Tim and Susan Simon for housing us while working on this project; and to our Creator for leading us to the Rock People so that their protective and healing message can be heard.

The faces on the Rock People in this book are genuine creations of nature.

A portion of proceeds are donated to heal and protect the Earth.

Printed in the USA on eco-friendly FSC certified paper. FSC

Rock People Press
P.O. Box 8105
Ann Arbor, Mi 48107
www.therockpeople.net

Library of Congress Cataloging-in-Publication Data
ISBN 978-0-615-28071-4

This book is dedicated to the Native Americans
who taught us to respect all creation.

There once was a little girl named Nae-Nae

who lived in a crowded city with busy streets and tall buildings. More than anything, Nae-Nae longed for trips away from the noise of the city.

Nae-Nae's favorite trip was to the lake house that her family rented every July. Nae-Nae, her mother, her father, and her sister loaded up their family jeep and headed north toward the lake.

Through her car windows, Nae-Nae watched the landscape change from tall city buildings

to open fields and farms.

Nae-Nae squealed in excitement when their jeep made its final turn onto the tree-lined lane leading to the lake house. As soon as her father unlocked the cottage door, Nae-Nae ran through the house and down the deck stairs leading to the beach.

Nae-Nae bent down along the edge of the shore to feel the lake. As the waves caressed her hands, Nae-Nae looked around to see that everything was just as she had remembered. Seagulls flew overhead; beach grass leaned in the wind; and the lake stretched out to the horizon.

Nae-Nae treasured her long summer days at the lake. She would build sandcastles;

disappear in the tall reeds along the shore;

and, with her daddy at her side, conquer the big waves of the lake.

But most of all, Nae-Nae loved to collect rocks scattered along the beach. Nae-Nae thought rocks were fascinating. There were so many sizes, shapes, and colors. Nae-Nae even imagined the rocks as her friends.

One day, while searching the beach for rocks, Nae-Nae discovered something amazing. It was a rock that appeared to be gazing right up at her!

Nae-Nae bent down to take a closer look. The rock had two eyes and a mouth. Nae-Nae picked up the rock, and placed it in the palm of her hand. To Nae-Nae's surprise it was now looking eye to eye with her! As they studied each other, Nae-Nae saw that the rock had a gentle and friendly face. But Nae-Nae also sensed there was something the rock wanted to say to her.

Looking around Nae-Nae spied another face. And then another! The more she looked the more faces on rocks she saw.

Nae-Nae ran to the house and called her family down to the beach to show them her discovery. "Look at the faces on these rocks!" she said.

That night Nae-Nae put three of the rocks she collected on the night-stand next to her bed. When Nae-Nae's mother came to tuck her into bed she ran her fingers over the face of one of the rocks. "Mommy," Nae-Nae asked, "who are these rock people?" "Scoot over sweetheart and I will tell you," her mother said. Once they were snuggled together under the blankets her mother began.

"Today, honey, you discovered the Rock People. When I was just about your age I discovered the Rock People too. My mother and father used to bring me to this very same lake house every summer. The bed you are sleeping in was my bed too. The day I discovered the Rock People my mother told me a legend about them. Now I will tell you."

THE LEGEND OF THE ROCK PEOPLE

In the beginning we lived in harmony with Earth.

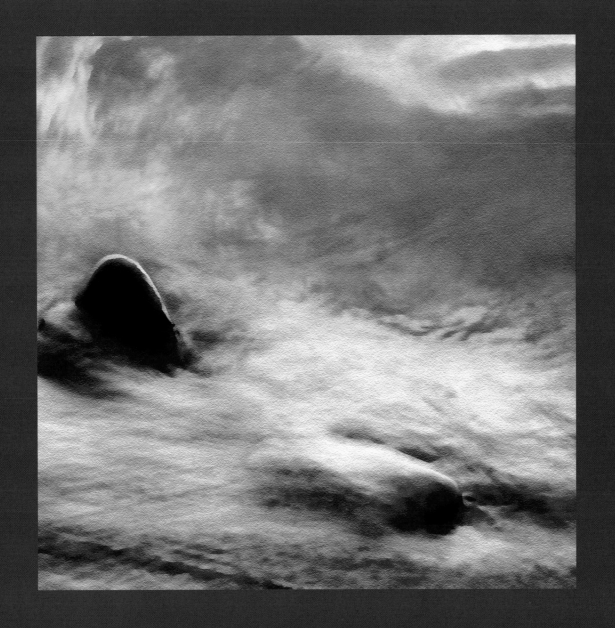

Still, The Great Creator sensed that one day we could harm Earth. Earth would need guardians.

So The Great Creator made the Rock People to protect Earth.

The Rock People were perfect for the job. They lay on Earth's surface where they could feel our footsteps on the land.

For thousands of years our footsteps were gentle on Earth. So the Rock people snoozed as Earth rotated peacefully.

But over time we grew careless. Footsteps, which once tiptoed gently on Earth, were marching recklessly everywhere.

Pristine forests were stripped of trees; fresh air became thick with smog; and fresh water became littered with trash.

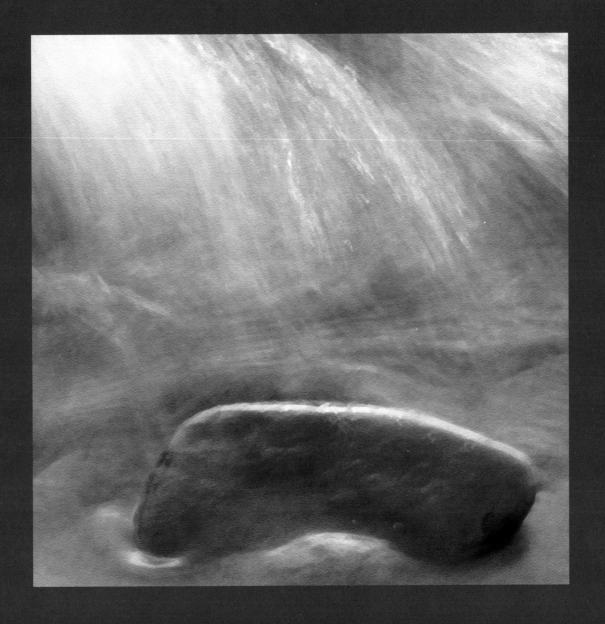

The Rock People sensed Earth's pain. Earth needed their help. But what could they do? The Rock People realized that they needed to communicate with us.

To do this, they began to transform themselves,
etching faces right on their rugged surfaces.

To communicate that Earth was hurt they formed
faces of sadness, pain, and fear.

*To communicate how to heal Earth they formed
faces of compassion, hope, and love.*

The Rock People are communicating with us.
Not everyone hears them. But those that do
hear them have the power to heal Earth.

Yawning, Nae-Nae said, "Mommy, I think the Rock People were trying to tell me something today." Slipping out of bed, her mother kissed Nae-Nae's forehead and said, "Yes, sweetheart, I'm sure they were."

Nae-Nae woke up early the next morning. Quietly tiptoeing out of the cottage, she went down to the beach to visit the Rock People.

Looking down, Nae-Nae saw a rock wearing a sad face. It made Nae-Nae think about the pollution in her city. Earth was hurt and that made Nae-Nae sad.

Nae-Nae then saw a rock with a soothing face. It made her realize there were things she could do to help Earth. Nae-Nae felt comforted.

Holding the Rock People in her hand, Nae-Nae sensed what they were saying to her:

Live gently with the Earth.